Amish Gardens: Amish Buggy Ride

Copyright © Samantha Fisher 2018

All rights reserved. No part of this publication may be reproduced, digitally stored, or transmitted in any form without written permission from the author.

TABLE OF CONTENTS

PROLOGUE
CHAPTER ONE
CHAPTER TWO
CHAPTER THREE
CHAPTER FOUR
CHAPTER FIVE
CHAPTER SIX
CHAPTER SEVEN
CHAPTER EIGHT
CHAPTER NINE
CHAPTER TEN

Author Note:

This book is a work of fiction, set against the backdrop of a fictional town. Characters, names, places, and incidents are the product of the author's imagination. There is no intentional similarity between the fictional contents of this *Happily-Ever-After* book and any actual people, places, or incidents. Any similarities are purely coincidental and out of the control of the author. Because this is a work of fiction, the author has taken creative license to create the characters and setting to provide the best entertaining experience for the reader. Any inaccuracies relating to the authenticity of the Amish lifestyle are due to creative license and should not be taken as text-book facts on the Amish. To do so, would destroy the fictional quality that the author hopes to provide.

Thank you for your faithful readership.

PROLOGUE

Casey Harper clenched her birth records to her chest as if they were a treasure to be guarded. In a way, they were; at least they were to her. They were her birthday present. A gift she'd waited twenty-one long years to have. Her heart pounded as she imagined what the pages might contain. Did she have some long-lost relatives who would accept her after all these years?

Did they even know about her?

Truthfully, she'd given up that dream years ago after seeing countless kids adopted. They'd always pass her by, and the other kids had teased her that no family wanted her because she was Amish.

There had been a lot of talk over the years about her being Amish, and though she didn't know how the rumors had gotten started, she suspected they might have come from a loose-lipped employee who was present at her birth. She'd suffered a lot of ridicule over the years from the other kids in the facility, and she'd gotten a few bruises and two cracked ribs defending herself, but it had been worth it. It wasn't like they were accusing her of anything; but they were disrespecting her, and somehow, that felt worse.

She'd seen kids come and go in the state-run home that felt more like a prison than a home. It had remained her prison for eighteen years until they let her outside the gate with not much more than the clothes on her back and the same, ninety-day rent voucher and two-year scholarship for college they gave each kid when they were deemed no longer to be the responsibility of the state. Between her job in the housekeeping department at the Holiday Inn and her classes, she'd managed to keep herself occupied until this day.

Casey had had one goal her entire life; to get ahold of her birth records. Though she'd had to leave them behind when she'd been pushed out of the gate three years ago, she'd been more determined than ever to get her hands on them.

She'd all but convinced herself that the only reason her family hadn't come to claim her was that they were Amish. From what she knew of the Amish, they didn't use phones, and they kept themselves closed up from the rest of the world.

Since her records were sealed like most kids who ended up at the orphanage, the state would not have had the authority to contact any family members on her behalf without her mother's permission. All she knew for certain was that the woman had died in the infirmary at the orphanage before the ambulance had arrived. Because of that, she might not have had the chance to give them those permissions.

Casey stood outside the gate to the orphanage with her eyes closed trying to imagine what might have brought her birth-mother to this place. Was she young and scared? Then her mind wandered to something she'd never really thought about; did she have a *father?* She'd always dreamed about her mother but hadn't ever given any thought to who her father might be.

Casey shrugged away the lump in her throat and breathed in the crisp, autumn air. She was finally free. So why couldn't she bring herself to open the envelope? She'd come to terms with her mother's death many years ago. Still, finding out her name and other things about her would make her *real.*

She walked toward the bus stop, holding her gift close to her. Though she was scared, she *had* to know what was inside. Her hands shook as she turned the envelope over and lifted the flap. She'd waited so long, and the anticipation had built in her so intensely, she worried the contents would only be a let-down.

There was only one way to find out.

She pulled a single page from the envelope and gazed at her birth-mother's name; Katie Lapp.

Her father, on the other hand, was listed as *unknown.* The only relative she mentioned was her older sister, Lila Yoder, who owned a B&B with her husband, just outside of the city. Yoder?

Under the description of nationality, Katie was listed as German, with the word *Amish* in parenthesis.

So, it was true; Casey's mother was *Amish.*

CHAPTER ONE

Casey Adjusted her backpack, the weight of it making her shoulder ache. The long, ribbon of country road that led to her *aunt's* B&B was barren. She'd foolishly thought to hitchhike to avoid paying for a cab, but there wasn't a car in sight.

She listened to the birds as she walked alongside the grassy shoulder beside the scorching asphalt, knowing it wouldn't be long before they would fly south for the winter. She would miss them, but autumn was one of her favorite times of the year. Breathing in the sweet aroma of the multicolored maple leaves, she stopped walking long enough to grab her water bottle from the side pocket of her backpack and took a long swig. The afternoon sun was warm against her back, and she could feel it burning her skin. By the time she reached the B&B, she would surely be overheated and sunburned.

She tried to keep her emotions in check even though it made her angry to think she had relatives living only a few miles away her entire life. She could hardly blame them—unless they knew about her and didn't try to help her, but she would meet them first, and then decide. She was determined to give them a chance—just in case they were no more aware of her than she was of them all this time.

Over the years, she'd heard conflicting stories about the Amish, but she'd never met one. She'd watched them on TV, and had seen a few in town on the occasions when they were outside the orphanage grounds on a field trip. But none had attended the public schools. As far as she knew, they had their own school and didn't go past eighth grade. If her mother had no husband, it was no wonder she wouldn't have been able to keep her even if she had lived. She would have had no way of supporting a child with so little education.

Casey pushed down the negative thoughts. She had never been one to be able to look at the positive side of things. Her teachers had always accused her of having a chip on her shoulder, and in some ways, she supposed they were right. She'd felt cheated out of the things in life that most people took for granted.

Things like *family*.

A strange noise from behind her caused her to turn in time to see a horse-driven buggy come up over the rise.

She flagged down the driver and waited until he slowed the buggy. Strangely, Casey found his primitive look almost appealing. Dark blond hair fell beneath his straw hat, and his baby-blue dress shirt was rolled at the sleeves, the color complimenting his sun-kissed face. His chiseled jaw was peppered with a light shadow of whiskers, his blue eyes smiling as wide as the grin that crossed his full lips. He looped a finger in one of his suspenders and stretched it a little and then rested his hand on the leg of his black dress pants.

Not bad—hope he's not related!

He cleared his throat, and Casey lifted her eyes to meet his; had he noticed she'd been staring at him?

"Where are you headed?" he asked, his accent heavy. "The only thing down this road is the Yoder B&B."

She nodded, returning his smile. "I know; that's where I'm headed."

"Then you must be looking to rent a room, or you're applying for the job, *jah?*"

She paused. Were they hiring? She couldn't ask for a more perfect cover than that. If she told them she was there for the job, then she didn't have to reveal her identity right away. That would give her time to get to know them and decide if they had left her in the orphanage *on purpose.*

"Yes!" she said, crossing her fingers behind her back, the way she did whenever she fibbed. "I'm applying for the job."

"*Frau* Yoder's *dochder,* Amy, broke her leg last week and they haven't been able to get anyone to fill in—not with the harvest season in full swing. Everyone is busy on their own farms this time of the year. *Frau* Yoder will be happy you're coming to her rescue."

I hope it's the other way around and she's coming to my rescue!

"Would you like a ride there?" he asked with a smile. "It's another three or four miles. On foot, that could take you more than an hour in this hot sun. *Mei* horse is not much faster, but at least it will give your feet a little bit of rest and keep you from burning in the sun."

She agreed it did seem like she'd been walking for at least half the day, though, in reality, it probably hadn't been more than an hour or so. The thought of finding out who the handsome stranger was, held some appeal for her.

"Yes," she said, smiling at the handsome Amish guy. "I'd like a ride."

"I'm Caleb Yoder," he said.

"I'm Casey—Harper," she said, suddenly questioning who she really was. At the orphanage, they named you the same way hurricanes were named, and they happened to be on the letter *H* when she'd been born. Was she really Casey *Lapp*—the same as her mother—or perhaps whatever her father's last name was. No, she was an orphan—a no-named orphan.

She flung her backpack up to his waiting hand with a sigh and waited for him to tuck it under the seat before attempting to climb into the buggy. He surprised her by reaching for her hand to assist her. Once she was seated next to him on the small bench, she found herself having to stare out of the tiny window beside her to avoid his gaze. His leg, which was touching hers was warming her and tossing around the butterflies that suddenly stirred in her stomach.

"Are you related to the woman who runs the B&B?" she asked, worrying they might be related.

Please say no!

"*Jah,*" he answered. "She is *mei* second cousin."

"Oh," Casey said, not meaning to sound so disappointed.

"We are related only by marriage; *mei vadder* and her husband are—were—cousins, but she's a widow now, so I look after her."

Casey did the calculating in her head. By his explanation, that wouldn't make him related to her by blood, and that eased her conscience some for the immediate attraction she had to him. Though she'd heard Amish married their distant cousins, she still felt better knowing she and Caleb weren't related—not that they would be getting married or anything like that. She was too young to be thinking about such things—and much too confused about who she was. But dating—that was something she'd not taken the time for yet, even though she'd had plenty of offers.

Before she'd had much time to enjoy the passing landscape, Caleb stopped his buggy in front of the most charming house she'd ever seen—aside from in her dreams.

Casey stared at the blue and white clapboard home with the wraparound porch. The flowers along the trellis and in hanging pots made it very inviting. It was a place like she'd dreamed about most of her life. She'd always wanted a porch like that where she could sit on hot summer evenings sipping lemonade and running in the grass chasing after lightning bugs. But all she got was one small window at the orphanage with a hole in the screen big enough to let in the mosquitoes.

The sign in front said *Yoder B&B; your home away from home.* A smaller sign hanging from the bottom said *Vacancy.* If they were Amish, Casey wouldn't know it by looking at the place.

She'd checked online, and there was only one B&B listed under the name Yoder, and the numbers above the front door matched the address they'd put in her file. The file that never got finished because her birth-mother had died before they could get any more information out of her. All she knew was the woman's name was Lila, and she was her birth-mother's sister. She'd always thought it was selfish of her birth-mother to sign a form stating that she was not to be placed with a family member, but perhaps she was too young to understand at that time and only thought to protect the secret of her pregnancy. Still, it was the least she could have done for her daughter before she died.

Casey stayed inside the buggy staring at the house, a million thoughts crowding her mind. Caleb hopped down and walked around to her side and offered his hand to her again.

She forced a smile, feeling suddenly sick to her stomach. She was about to meet her mother's sister, and she had no idea what she would say to the woman. She couldn't blurt out who she was—she'd come across as a crazy person. Why hadn't she thought this through? She was here, and she couldn't back out without having to explain to Caleb. Funny that she'd never been afraid of anything in her life—so why was she so nervous now?

"The job will come with free room and board if you need it," Caleb said.

The job—right—the job; that's why she was here. At least, that was her cover.

She forced another smile and took his hand, the warmth of it causing her to blush.

"You will like it here," Caleb continued, oblivious to her shakiness. "I have a can of milk in the back and some butchered beef to deliver around the back of the *haus,* but you go on up to the front door and introduce yourself."

Casey stood there taking in the house and the flowers, even the squirrels chasing each other around the large oak tree in the front yard. She smiled, feeling a sense of love pouring from the place. She could see the flawless care taken with the yard. Not a single weed sprang from the flower bed.

The screen door swung open with a squeak, an older woman with graying hair tucked behind a black bonnet stood there smiling as she wiped her hands on a black apron that covered the full length of her long, navy dress.

"I see you've met Caleb," she said, her accent thicker than his. "*Kume,* sit on the porch; I'll get some lemonade, and we can visit."

Lemonade on the porch? It was just as she'd imagined.

"I have fresh cookies from the oven," she said, eyeing Casey as if she knew her. "I'll bring them with the lemonade. You've had a long journey, *jah?*"

Casey nodded; it had been a long journey getting here. And she had to admit; there was a strange familiarity in the woman's eyes—as if she'd seen them in her dreams—when she was a child.

"I'm Lila Yoder," the woman said.

"I'm Casey," was all she could spit out while her backpack slid from her shoulder to the floor of the porch with a thud.

"Let me take that for you," Lila said kindly. "I can put it inside for you while we talk."

"I can take it," she said. "It's a little bit heavy."

Lila waved a hand at her. "Nonsense; you're my guest."

Casey was unable to take her eyes off the woman, who smiled warmly and welcomed her to sit on the porch swing.

So you're my Aunt Lila!

CHAPTER TWO

Caleb went around behind the B&B and let himself in through the service door at the back of the kitchen to put the milk can inside the big walk-in refrigerator. The Bishop was lenient with his community about using electricity for a business as long as the living quarters for the business owners remained without it. For that reason, *Frau* Yoder and her daughter, Amy, lived in the *dawdi haus* on the back of the property. Normally such a house was reserved for grandparents, but the eldest of the Yoder clan had passed away.

"Who's here with you?" Amy said, startling him.

"I picked up a young *Englisher* walking along the road on the way here," he answered. "She's talking to your *mudder* about the job."

Amy sneered. "You *picked her up* along the road? What is she—homeless?"

"I don't know; I didn't ask her!"

"Where did she come from?" Amy asked, trying to lean far enough to look through the house to the front porch.

"I don't know," Caleb said, removing his work gloves. "I didn't ask her."

"We can't hire a homeless stranger," Amy complained, adjusting her leg with the cast on it.

"Your *mudder* seems to like her, and I thought she was pleasant."

Amy smirked. "Judging by the smile on your face, she must be pleasant to *look at.*"

"*Jah,*" he said. "She is—in a plain sort of way."

"You don't think she's trying to pass herself off as Amish or Mennonite—to get the job, do you?"

Caleb laughed. "I don't think so, but if you're that worried about her, why don't you go see for yourself!"

Amy curled her lip and reached for her crutches. "Maybe I will."

Caleb put a hand on her crutches and flashed her a stern look. "Your *mudder* can handle her business, and you're supposed to be resting that leg. Didn't the doctor tell you to stay off it unless it was necessary?"

She huffed. "My leg is none of your business, and it is necessary for me to get up; I need some fresh air. It's too stuffy in the *haus,* and the doctor told me to get as much fresh air as possible."

Caleb scowled at her. "You are stubborn, Cousin."

"We're not cousins," Amy barked.

Caleb knew the reason behind her comment. She wanted him to court her, and he would not do anything to encourage her. He would continue to call her cousin all day just to keep her from trying to sink her hooks in him. She was immature and gossipy, and that was not the sort of woman he would choose to be his *fraa*. Put plainly; they were not a good match.

Amy had done everything she could to make everyone at the youth singings believe the two of them had been promised to each other, while he did everything he could to keep his distance from her. Right now, she was acting jealous—another trait he didn't care for. He'd done his best to make her understand he wasn't interested in her just short of being rude, which he would never do. Unfortunately for him, she didn't take hints well.

He excused himself politely so he could get the packages of butchered beef into the walk-in freezer before it thawed in the back of his buggy from the hot sun. That, and he wanted to sneak another glance at Casey. She was very beautiful, but he'd do his best to keep his thoughts to himself unless he wanted Amy unleashing her fury on the poor girl before she got a chance to secure the job. He wasn't certain what it was about her, but somehow, he had the feeling she really needed to be here.

When he finished, he went back around the front to say goodbye to the widow—and to Casey.

Lord, make a way for Casey to get the job here at the B&B if it is your will.

Caleb wasn't sure why exactly he'd prayed for her to get hired on, but he supposed it was partly for selfish reasons. He couldn't quite pinpoint the reason, but he wanted the chance to get to know her better.

"Are you finished?" Lila asked him.

He nodded, glancing shyly toward Casey.

"Will you join us for some cool lemonade?" Lila asked.

He darted his glance between them noting they seemed to be getting along nicely.

"I don't want to intrude," he said, hesitating. "But you know I can't pass up your lemonade or your molasses cookies."

She had already gotten up from her chair and began pouring him a glass. He noticed she'd brought out an extra glass—as if she'd expected him to interrupt them before he left. Then again, she did always have the treat ready for him after each of his weekly deliveries. She was one of his best customers, and not only did he get a fresh batch of cookies to take home with him, he usually got a few chickens and several dozen eggs as part of his payment.

"When you finish, would you mind going out to the hen house and gathering your own eggs today?" she asked. "With Amy laid up, I haven't had the chance to get them for you."

He nodded, not wanting to answer for fear he'd spit cookie crumbs all over the porch.

Lila picked up the tray and smiled at him. "Why don't you take Casey with you; we're finished here, and she'll need to know where to go and how to pluck them from under the hens come morning time. Since she'll be working here, that will be part of her responsibilities. I have to get two rooms ready for a couple of guests who should be arriving in about an hour."

"I'd be happy to help in any way I can," Caleb offered with a warm smile. "Congratulations on the job!"

Casey smiled shyly. "Thank you."

Casey followed Caleb into the barnyard where chickens ran freely near a cute little coop that was a small version of the main house, complete with a wraparound porch. It had been painted white with blue shutters like the main house and even had flower boxes under the windows.

She giggled, feeling enchanted by the little cottage. "That's adorable! It's like a little doll house for the chickens."

"Abner, Lila's husband made chicken coops for a living, but he made this one special for her—to match the *haus,*" Caleb said. "He was a *gut mann* with great talent."

"I've never seen anything like it."

Caleb grabbed a basket hanging from a little hook near the door and opened it, holding it open for her. Little walking ramps went up to the two front windows, and she supposed that was how the chickens went in and out of the little house. Once inside, Casey jumped and squealed when one of the hens squawked and flew across the coop to the other side; she grabbed Caleb's arm instinctively and ducked behind him.

He chuckled. "She won't hurt you; they are used to me, but you probably startled her more than she did you."

Shaking, Casey still clutched his arm. The hens continued to squawk and flap their wings, causing her to jump again.

"You will get used to them, and they will settle down once they get to know you," he said, reaching out a hand and petting one of the hens. "They are very gentle, but they startle easy, so don't make any sudden movements or they will try to fly."

"They can't fly?"

He smiled. "*Nee,* you have to keep their wings clipped, or they will roost in the trees, and then you will be forever searching for the eggs, most of which will end up smashed on the ground or in the belly of foxes and other animals."

Casey gulped when he tucked an arm around her waist and urged her toward the nesting boxes that lined the walls.

"Watch what I do," he said, reaching under the hen. When he pulled his hand out, he had a brownish-red egg in his hand.

Casey smiled when he put it in the basket.

"Now you try this one here."

She put her hand out toward the chicken and hesitated.

"They don't bite, do they?" she asked, her voice and hand a little shaky.

He suppressed a chuckle. "*Nee,* they might act like they will peck you with their beak, but it doesn't hurt."

Casey swiped her hand back and stood even closer to him.

"I don't want them to attack me!"

He peeled her hands off from around him and held them tight, drawing her nearer. The warmth of his hands sent tingles all the way up her arms, his closeness making her dizzy.

"Somehow you don't strike me as the type of girl who is afraid of anything."

He was wrong; her tough exterior was all an act. Her insides were so tossed around, even her knees knocked. She'd never let something this trivial make her weak in the knees. Was it possible it was Caleb's closeness that frightened her?

He moved both their hands slowly toward the brownish-red hen and dipped their hands underneath.

"I feel the egg!" she said.

"Grab it!" he said.

She grabbed the egg and pulled her hand out from under the hen, suddenly realizing he'd taken his hand away, but he was still so close to her she could feel an exhilarating spark of warmth emanating from him. It was distracting her from her fear of gathering the eggs, and she supposed that was the whole idea.

She put the egg in the basket along with the one Caleb had gotten, and she smiled, feeling proud of herself.

"I knew you could do it," he said with a smile. "Get another one; this time, do it by yourself."

Casey hesitated, and Caleb pulled her close to him using the arm that he'd tucked around her at the small of her back. It caused her to draw in a dreamy breath. She'd never been kissed before; would he kiss her? He looked down at her, his eyes focusing on her mouth. She wanted him to kiss her so much her breath heaved.

A clunking noise preceded bright sunshine that made them squint when the door to the coop swung open. A loud gasp brought their attention to the doorway.

"What are you doing, Caleb Yoder?" Amy squealed.

CHAPTER THREE

Caleb let go of Casey and scowled at Amy, who was struggling with her crutches and leaning against the door for support.

"She was afraid of the chickens, and I was showing her how to gather the eggs," he said, clearing his throat and putting even more distance between himself and Casey. The last thing he needed was to have his gossipy cousin tattling on him and twisting the truth.

Amy twisted up her face. "It looked to me like you were kissing her!"

I might have if you hadn't interrupted.

"*Ach,* mind your own business, Cousin, and go back inside before you break your other leg worrying about what I'm doing!"

She huffed. "Stop calling me *Cousin!*" she said, her teeth gritting.

He ignored her demand and turned to Casey, who was now standing as far away from him as she could in the small space.

"Casey," he addressed her. "This is *mei* cousin, Amy."

"It's nice to meet you," Casey said.

Amy growled at the two of them and turned around so fast, she nearly fell. She hobbled away, and Caleb let the door swing closed again.

"Now, where were we?" he asked. "I believe it's your turn to get one of those eggs on your own."

He motioned for her to try the next hen roosting quietly. It squawked and lifted its wings, causing her to squeal and pull her hand away.

"Try it again," he urged her. "They have to get used to you if you're going to work here; you'll have to gather the eggs every morning."

She winced, and it made him chuckle.

"It's easy for you to say," she said. "You've probably been doing this all your life."

He nodded. "It's true. Even the young *kinner* get the eggs—practically from the time they learn to walk. They are usually with their *mudders,* but they do learn from a young age."

Casey folded her arms and frowned. "I must look like a big baby to you!"

Caleb bit his bottom lip and shook his head. "*Nee*, you look like an *Englisher* who has never gathered eggs—except for maybe from the supermarket?"

Casey giggled. "I thought that was where eggs came from—neat little cartons in the dairy section at the grocery store!"

"For *Englishers, jah,* but here on the Amish farms, we still have to get them straight from the chickens. You will see when you taste them for the first time how much fresher they are."

She giggled again. "I'd have to say getting them straight from the chicken is mighty fresh."

Caleb motioned back toward the chickens roosting in the nesting boxes. "What do you say we give this another try?"

Casey nodded. Truthfully, this was more fun than she'd had her entire life, but she might still play the *helpless female* just for another chance to be close to Caleb.

"Okay," she grumbled playfully. "But stay close—just in case one of them attacks me!"

Caleb laughed, but she suppressed it, pushing out her lower lip.

"You can do better than that," he said. "I have confidence in you."

His comment struck her as funny. She'd never felt anyone had confidence in her. It was something she could get used to.

"Thank you," she said with a smile.

She could see in his eyes that he understood.

Reaching underneath one of the hens with caution, Casey felt the egg. Excited she'd gotten it, she grabbed it with gusto, bursting it open by accident. "Oh no!" she squealed.

Caleb snickered. "That sounded like an egg cracking!"

"It broke," she whined. She removed her hand from under the hen, egg yolk dripping from her fingers. "Oh, that's disgusting."

"It's happened to all of us a time or two," Caleb reassured her. "Just flick your hand toward the back of the coop and go in for another one!"

She stood there, the egg still dripping between her fingers. "You really want me to try that again?"

He nodded. "*Jah,* only next time, don't squeeze it when you grab it. It's not a rock!"

"Really?" she said with a smirk. "Because I thought it was a smooth rock when I felt it under that hen."

She flicked the egg yolk from her hand the way he told her to and then went in for another one. She cupped it gently in her hand and retrieved it. "I did it!"

He moved toward her hand and chuckled. "Not yet; it's not safe in the basket yet."

She plunked it into the basket, and it cracked against the one that was in there. "Oops; sorry!"

Caleb shook his head and laughed. "They didn't break, but let's try again. Watch me once more."

He tucked his hand under one of the hens and pulled out the egg and then placed it down into the basket, not letting go until it was clear of the other eggs. Casey mimicked his every move and then finally got it. She tried several more times until Caleb cautioned her to stop.

"This is enough for me to take with me. We don't want the hens to get into a different routine. Most of them only lay one egg a day, and that's usually in the morning. You'll need the eggs in the mornings for the large breakfasts you'll prepare."

"What if there aren't any guests?" she asked.

"You'll still cook for the *familye* and the staff, which consists of yourself—and me, occasionally. I fix a lot of stuff around here, so if you notice anything that needs repairing, put it on the list for me. It's in the mudroom on the chalkboard."

"Okay," she said. "I'll do that."

Caleb looked into the basket and smiled. "You've got yourself the makings for a nice salad topping. Boil these up for you and the ladies."

"What about you?" she asked. "Weren't these yours?"

"I don't need them today. Pick some greens from the garden—maybe a tomato or two and some carrots and celery, and you've got yourself a nice summer salad."

"They grow all that? Here?" she asked.

Caleb held the door for her and closed it behind them. Then he took her arm and led her to the garden. Her entire arm tingled from his strong touch. Was he this way with all women, or just the clumsy—what had he called her? An Englisher.

They walked between the rows of the garden while he pointed out potato plants, carrots, celery, the tomatoes, and even spinach—one of her favorites.

"We grow a lot of root vegetables that we keep in the cellar during the winter months. Others that don't keep as well, the ladies in the community get together and have canning bees."

Casey chuckled. "They can—bees?"

Caleb chuckled. "And people say we Amish live under a rock!"

Truth-be-told, she had been living under a rock most of her life. At the orphanage, she'd been very sheltered. Since she'd been on her own, she hadn't had the time to indulge in much TV or the news or even learn how to surf the internet until she began her classes. She didn't even own a cell phone.

"We have what is called a working *bee,* which is where everyone gathers together in one spot and works on a project—I suppose in some ways it's like a beehive."

Interesting!

"You will learn to sew quilts and can vegetables and make jam," he said. "That is—if you want to learn such things."

"Oh, I do want to learn—all of it."

She didn't want to tell him she was eager to learn the things from her heritage that she'd been deprived of while living in the orphanage. She wasn't ready to reveal her identity—not yet. Maybe she never would—she didn't know just yet. There would be plenty of time to worry about that now. Right now, God had dropped a job in her lap that would allow her to get to know her family without the pressure of possible rejection from them. She didn't want to think about that possibility. But somehow, they didn't seem like the type of people who would do that— except Amy. She had a mean-streak—the kind of mean like the bullies in the orphanage. Was she simply crabby because her leg hurt? Casey remembered how crabby her cracked ribs had made her. Perhaps she would make an extra effort to be kind to Amy hoping it would win her over in time.

"You could do some picking now if you'd like," Caleb said, interrupting her thoughts. "It might score some points with your boss—not that you need to. She seems happy with you. I've never seen her take to an *Englisher* that fast—she might just make you one of the *familye* before long."

Casey felt her heart thumping hard and fast. How could she deceive such a woman? Would she kick her out of the family once she learned Casey's secret?

She ignored her inner prompting to blurt out the truth and began picking vegetables from the garden—enough to make a large salad for dinner. She wasn't sure how much she would be doing on her own, but she hoped she'd be working closely alongside *Aunt Lila*.

I wish I wasn't such a coward; I would tell her now and take my lumps if that's what I need to do.

The truth was, Casey was a terrible coward and feared rejection more than most anything. She supposed it stemmed from being given up at birth and never getting adopted by any family.

Lord, let Aunt Lila adopt me; don't let her turn me away when she learns the truth about me.

Caleb touched her arm. "Are you alright?"

She hadn't noticed the tears that clouded her vision until now. "Um—yeah, I must be allergic to something out here."

He let out a sneeze. "It's probably the Marigolds planted around the tomatoes; the pollen in them seems to get to me too."

Thankfully, he'd given her an excuse to diffuse her mistake; it was probably best if she kept her thinking and worrying to herself from here on out.

"Are you ever coming in the *haus?*" Amy hollered from the kitchen door. "I need you to fix the latch on this cupboard; it fell on my foot and nearly broke all *mei* toes!"

Caleb looked toward the back door of the B&B and sighed. He forced a smile and nodded. "I'll be there in a minute."

Casey rolled her eyes. "She seems spoiled."

"She hasn't had an easy life," Caleb said. "Her *mudder's schwester* disappeared just before Amy was born; when they found out about her, she was in a morgue, and there was evidence she'd died in childbirth."

Casey felt her breath hitch, though she hadn't meant to.

Caleb ignored her and went on with his story. "Cousin Lila has spent the last twenty-one years searching for her *schwester's* child. Amy's been jealous of the child her whole life because of it."

Casey felt heat rise in her cheeks; the child she'd been searching for was *her*.

"Lila doesn't know what happened to her sister's baby?"

Caleb shrugged. "Her *familye* wasn't given any information. They said that if there was a child, he or she wouldn't surface until the child turned twenty-one, which they said is the legal age to get his or her birth records. Lila has been eagerly waiting all these years for the child to come looking for its *familye."*

Casey couldn't breathe; her heart pounded so hard she could hear it. Suddenly everything began to spin, and spots twinkled before her eyes. She felt her knees give out from under her and knew she was falling, but Caleb cradled her in his arms. That was the last thing she remembered before she felt nothing. Her eyes closed against the stress and she drifted into darkness.

CHAPTER FOUR

Casey's lashes fluttered, but she couldn't focus on anything. The room was too dark to see. "Momma—where are you?" she called out half asleep, panic shaking her voice.

"Keep calm and rest," a familiar woman's voice cooed her. "You're safe, but you gave us quite a scare."

She bolted upright, still a little groggy; she knew that voice—that accent. Had she been dreaming?

"What happened?"

The strike of a match followed by a light glow and the smell of sulfur brought her back to reality. She was at the B&B, and Lila was fussing with the quilt, tucking it back around her and urging her to lie back down.

"You fainted in the garden with Caleb; you don't remember?"

Yes, Caleb; I think he carried me into the house.

She relaxed against the feather pillow without answering and let the warmth of the quilt comfort her while Lila continued to fuss over her. It was all coming back to her now. Caleb had told her how hard Lila had tried to find her. Tears filled her eyes, and she was grateful the room was dimly-lit. Her heart sang at the thought of it; she had a family. Her only problem now would be to figure out a tactful way of approaching Lila about it.

Exhaustion overtook her, and she drifted in and out of sleep, but she picked up bits and pieces of the conversation between her aunt and her hostile cousin.

"Why are you bothering with that *Englisher?*" Amy complained. "She's probably homeless and plans to rob us or something."

Casey felt a cool cloth against her forehead and a warm hand pushing back her hair.

"You worry too much," Lila whispered. "She needs us to help her."

"Like all the others?" Amy pressed. "She isn't one of the foster kids you've been taking in for as long as I can remember—she's too old."

"I think this one is exactly the right age," Lila said.

"*Mamm*, you've taken in one child after another my whole life, hoping each one would be your *schwester's kinner*, and none of them were."

Casey felt the quilt being tucked under her chin and the light from the lantern dimmed almost to pitch blackness.

"I believe this one is different," Lila said.

Their conversation ended, and Casey opened her eyes after they left the room. She was wide awake now and couldn't stop thinking about what her aunt said about her efforts at taking in foster kids to find her. It would seem that she meant a great deal to the woman; so why had she held back the truth from her instead of coming clean with it. Was it her fear of rejection that kept her silent? Surely the woman wouldn't reject her after searching for her all these years, would she? Unless Casey's being an *Englisher* would change her mind about her.

Perhaps in the morning, she would tell Lila the truth. For now, she was content with the way things were.

Caleb pushed his way through the kitchen door at the B&B. Casey could see in his eyes he was surprised to see her up and around, much less at the stove making breakfast. She turned off the flame beneath the coffee pot and pulled down a second cup from the cabinet next to her.

"How are you feeling this morning?" he asked, closing the space between them and touching her arm.

His closeness made her knees wobble; was he going to have that effect on her every time he was near?

"I'm feeling much better," she answered. "Thank you for bringing me inside—and for not letting me take a nose-dive into the dirt."

"I'm glad I was there to catch you, or you certainly would have gotten a face full of dirt!" he said.

"How do you take your coffee?" she asked.

"I like it straight from the pot—as strong as you can make it!"

"Well, then you'll probably like my coffee; I only know one way to make it—thick as mud!"

She poured him a cup and handed it to him; he sipped it and smiled. "That is the best *kaffi* I've had in a long time! Where did you learn to make *kaffi* like that?"

"From the…" her voice trailed off when she realized she was about to say she'd learned at the orphanage. From the time she could reach the stove, she was volunteering to work in the kitchen. It was the best way to keep the bullies away from her during their free time. As long as she was busy working in the kitchen and then serving and cleaning up afterward, she was able to keep out of trouble. "I um—taught myself. I read a lot."

That wasn't a lie; she did love cookbooks almost as much as she liked a good fairytale.

"Don't suppose you taught yourself how to make cinnamon streusel too, did you?"

"I can make maple coffee cake."

He sniffed the air. "Is that what I smell that has my mouth watering so much?"

Casey smiled and tilted open the oven to have a peek inside. "I believe it's done! Sit down, and I'll cut you a slice. It's best when it's fresh from the oven."

He wasted no time taking his coffee to the table and waiting for her to set the slice of coffee cake in front of him. He breathed in the steam from the warm treat, the icing dripping over the pecans and onto the plate. He sliced into it with his fork, bringing a large chunk to his lips. His eyes closed in unison with his lips over the forkful, followed by yummy noises as he chewed; he didn't open his eyes again until after he swallowed.

He sighed dreamily as he gazed upon Casey's waiting expression. "It melts in your mouth! Now, this is the sort of thing that makes a *mann* want to marry a woman."

Casey giggled shyly. She'd never given marriage or dating much thought. Most of her life had been spent worrying about survival; now, though, she was free to dream. She could certainly see herself marrying Caleb. He was kind and handsome, and he was easy to be around. But would he still be so interested when he learned her identity?

He shoveled another large piece into his mouth, repeating the process, looking as though he was falling in love with Casey over her amazing coffee cake, his smile warming her insides.

"Don't you have work to do?" Amy barked from the doorway of the kitchen.

Casey groaned inwardly. *Where did she come from?*

Caleb rose from his chair after shoving the last bite of his coffee cake into his mouth and took his dish to the sink. "I can take a hint," he said, flashing Casey an apologetic look. "You ladies have work to do and don't need me underfoot. I'll be in the barn fixing the hinges on the horse stall so Midnight won't be able to get out again."

Once Caleb was out of the house, Amy plopped into the nearest chair and glared at Casey, who'd begun to crack eggs into a mixing bowl.

"You're not fooling me!" Amy said with a snotty tone. "You might think you're fooling *mei mudder*—and even Caleb, but you don't fool me."

Casey gulped. "I'm not trying to *fool* anyone. I'm only trying to do my job here."

"Your job does not include hanging out with Caleb."

"I'm only here to do my job," Casey retorted. "Until you're well enough to be back on your feet."

"What will you do then?" Amy asked.

"I suppose I'll move on if I'm not longer needed here."

Amy scowled. "You're not needed here now—and you're not wanted either."

Casey finished scrambling the eggs. "Your mother seems to think otherwise."

"Well, you make sure you stay away from Caleb," Amy warned. "We're practically betrothed."

Casey looked up from the bowl of eggs before pouring them in the iron skillet. "Betrothed?"

Amy rolled her eyes. "You know—engaged—to be married!"

Keep telling yourself that, Cousin!

"That means he's off limits," Amy continued. "So stay away from him—I'm warning you!"

You're warning me? Or what—you'll beat me up with your crutches?

Anger filled Casey as she set down the bowl full of eggs and turned to Amy, tears welling up in her eyes. She'd gotten pushed around her whole life, and she was not about to put up with it from someone who was supposed to be her family. If she wasn't wanted here, she would happily leave now and forget the whole thing. She didn't need this from anyone; she was an adult now, and capable of walking away. When she was a kid in the orphanage, she didn't have a choice. She had to live there and had to put up with a certain amount of unfair treatment, but not anymore.

Amy scoffed and smiled. "Don't tell me the tough girl is going to cry. Well, maybe all those mean foster kids I had to put up with all my life made me tougher than you, *Englisher!*"

"I'm not an *Englisher!*" Casey blurted out.

"Oh don't tell me now you're going to try to pass yourself off as Amish!"

Tears dripped from Casey's eyes. "I *wish* your mother would have found me sooner—for both our sake!"

Amy's face drained of all its color. "You heard what we said when you were *pretending* to be asleep last night! I know better than to think you're my long-lost cousin."

Casey hadn't meant for the truth to come out this way, but now that it was out there, she would show Amy the papers.

"It's true," Casey pleaded. "I've got papers to prove it—from the orphanage, where I grew up only a few miles from here. My mother's name was Katie Lapp, and the records showed she had a sister, Lila Yoder, who ran a B&B and it gave this address. I'll get the records—I'll be right back."

Casey ran from the room, and up to the bedroom she'd stayed in last night to get the records from her backpack. Excitement made her smile; she was so relieved the truth was out and surprised at how easy it was to tell Amy everything. She closed the door to the cozy room her aunt told her would be her room as long as she stayed. It was quaint but humble, but most of all, it was homey. The handmade quilt on the bed was vibrant with color, the poster bed and dresser were hand-crafted, and the rocking chair in the corner was endearing—the sort of chair a mother would sit in to rock her baby to sleep. She went over to the window and looked out toward the barn; Caleb was walking the large black horse out to the corral. He was a good man—handsome and hard working. The sort of man a girl dreams of marrying.

Caleb's gaze lifted and he sent a wave toward her. She waved back and smiled, her heart racing as she remembered their near kiss in the chicken coop yesterday.

Lord, please don't let Caleb turn me away when he finds out who I really am. I like him, and I think he likes me too.

When Caleb returned to the barn, Casey went over to the closet to get her backpack. Panic filled her when she found her clothes had been hung up on hangers. The backpack lay in a heap on the floor, and she sank to her haunches to examine it. If they went through her things, they might have already found the envelope from the orphanage with her records in them.

She tore open the bag, but it was empty; she searched every pocket, but they were all empty. She went to the dresser and flung open the drawers. Her personal things had been put away in the top drawer, but the rest were empty.

Her head whipped around to the table next to the bed, her heart drumming against her ribs like a big bass drum in a marching band. She closed the space between her and the table, praying the envelope was in the small drawer. She flung it open, but an old Bible was the only thing in the drawer. She pulled the Bible from the drawer and collapsed onto the bed, clutching the book close to her. She began to sob. If Amy had taken the papers, she would never give them back. The girl was bitter and angry with her mother for taking in so many orphans over the years, and Casey gathered she'd felt neglected because of it. On the other hand, if Lila had them, she would say something to her, wouldn't she?

Amy appeared in her doorway. "What's the matter with you?"

Casey bolted upright on the bed and wiped away her tears. "Nothing!" she fibbed.

"Where are your papers proving you're *mei* cousin?" Amy asked in a snotty tone. "Or was it all a lie? If you think we have some inheritance for you or something, you're not getting anything from this pack of lies you've built up in your head."

"I'm not lying!" Casey retorted.

"There isn't anything here for you, so why don't you leave."

"I don't want anything from you—except maybe..." she let her voice fall, unable to finish her sentence. There was no point in telling Amy she wanted to be a family; it was apparent Amy wanted no part of it.

"Since you can't prove who you are," Amy sneered. "I guess you ought to get back to work because from where I'm standing, you're just the hired help."

Tears streamed from Casey's eyes; she would find those records if she had to upturn every inch of this house.

CHAPTER FIVE

Amy returned to the room where Casey felt suddenly out of place. As soon as her cousin had left the room, she began to pack her things. There was no point in staying; as soon as her aunt heard of her claim, she'd send her packing anyway. Might as well save her the trouble.

Amy startled her when she pushed her way clumsily through the bedroom door. She hobbled into the room and spotted the backpack sitting on the bed.

"Going somewhere?" Amy sneered.

Casey shrugged and kept her back to her cousin. "I just figured I'd save your mother the trouble and leave."

"Suit yourself," Amy said. "But before you go; she wants to see you. I wouldn't bother embarrassing yourself any more than you already have, so it's probably best if you don't try to tell her the same lies you told me. And don't worry; I'll keep it just between the two of us—so you can walk out of here with your dignity intact."

Casey pursed her lips. "That's very kind of you, but I'm capable of handling my life without your advice."

Amy chortled. "Really? Because from where I'm standing, you're a homeless liar without a leg to stand on, so why don't you slither out of here and crawl back under the rock you came from."

Casey could feel her blood boiling as she took an aggressive step toward Amy, her jaw clenched. "I came from the same bloodline you did, and one way or another, I intend to prove it."

She couldn't face her aunt now. She had to put some space between them and hope her aunt would understand once she returned with a new copy of her birth records. She jutted out her chin defiantly and threw her backpack over her shoulder, and then walked toward the door.

"That's right; leave!" Amy practically shouted. "I knew you were lying."

Casey groaned when she heard the clip-clop from a horse and buggy wheels grinding in the pavement from behind her.

Please don't be Caleb again.

The buggy pulled up alongside her, and she glanced at the large black horse she knew belonged to Caleb.

So we meet again," Caleb said. "Why didn't you tell me you were going into town? I could have given you a ride."

"I don't need a ride," she said, keeping her face forward and continuing to walk.

Caleb tapped the reins lightly to get his horse to walk slowly beside her.

Tears dripped down her cheeks, her eyes burned, and she could feel how puffy they were; she hated for Caleb to see her this way.

"Why the backpack?" he asked. "You aren't leaving, are you?"

Casey shuddered and sniffled. "That's the general idea! Amy practically kicked me out; it's obvious she doesn't want me there."

"Lila does!" Caleb said. "And I do!"

Casey stopped walking and looked up at him in the buggy.

"I find that hard to believe," she said, sniveling.

Caleb set the brake and hopped down. He pulled her into his arms, and that caused her to let go of a fresh batch of tears. Her shoulders shook from the anger and hurt she felt.

"It can't be all that bad, can it?" he asked.

"Amy hates me!"

Caleb smirked. "She hates everyone—even me!"

Casey shook her head. "No—she doesn't hate you; she thinks you're her *betrothed.*"

"*Ach,* she hates me because she can't have me," he assured her. "But she told you she was engaged to me to get under your skin. That's how she is. She's had a rough time, and she's taking it out on you."

"She blames me, but it wasn't my fault."

"Why would she blame you?" Caleb asked.

"Because I'm Katie Lapp's daughter!"

Caleb pulled into the cemetery and stopped the buggy near a set of grave markers lined up neatly beside a large oak tree.

"What are we doing here?" Casey asked, her voice shaky.

Caleb hopped down from the buggy and took her by the hand. "There's something you need to see."

"In a graveyard?" she asked, her heart pounding erratically.

She followed him as he walked along the path until he stopped and pointed to a plain grave marker. "I've brought Lila here to visit many times, but I think you need to visit too."

Her breath caught in her throat at the carving on the headstone.

Katie Lapp, beloved daughter, sister, and friend.

Casey sank to the grass and touched the headstone. "She died on my birthday!" She buried her face in her hands and began to sob. "Oh, Mamma, why did you have to leave me the way you did?"

Casey felt a warm hand on her shoulder. "I've heard the story so many times; I feel I know it by heart," Caleb said softly. "Do you want me to tell you, or would you rather hear it from your *Aenti* Lila?"

She sniffled. "I'd like to hear it now."

Caleb knelt in the grass beside Casey and put his arm around her and kissed the top of her head.

"Your *mudder* and *Aenti* Lila got into a fight because she left for her *rumspringa*—her time of running around before joining the church—just before Lila's wedding. A few months after, Lila got a letter from Katie telling her she was pregnant and asked for help. Lila was upset with her and shunned her for running off and getting pregnant out of wedlock. A few months after that, a couple of police officers showed up at the B&B and told Lila your *mudder* had died before they got her to the hospital. They told her that Katie had given birth to a child and had signed adoption papers in her eighth month of pregnancy and they could not legally give her any information about the child. Lila begged them to tell her; she even hired a lawyer. In the end, she took in as many foster kids as she could along the years. The kids she took in were always the same age as Katie's child would have been that year. She never knew if the child was a boy or a girl so she took in every kid the state would allow her to. She did everything she could to find you all these years. That's why you *have* to go back and tell Lila. You have no idea how happy you'll make her."

Casey's breath hitched. "Amy will tell her I'm lying."

"Then let's go get another copy of your records to show her," he said. "Amy can't keep taking them all. We'll get two copies, and I'll hold onto one; we'll do whatever we have to so you can prove who you are. Lila *needs* to know; I think it will finally give her the peace she's needed all these years. You have no idea the guilt she's suffered from turning her sister away. She blames herself that she couldn't raise you after Katie's death."

Casey paused to look into his eyes, a sincere kindness glowing in his expression. "Why would you help me like this? It's not your problem."

He pulled her hands into his and smiled, sending shivers right through her.

"Isn't it obvious?" he asked. "I think I'm falling for you, and if you're Amish, we can be together. That is—if you're interested in me, too."

Casey's heart sped up, and the butterflies in her stomach were going crazy. She was falling for him too and couldn't deny that he'd occupied her thoughts far more than her quest to find her family. She nodded and flashed him a smile. "Yes, I am. Do the Amish *date?*"

"*Jah,* they go for buggy rides," he said with a smile.

Casey let a giggle escape her lips and wiped the tears from her cheeks. "We've taken two of those already!"

He chuckled. "Yes, we have, so I guess that means—with your permission, of course, that we can go for an *official* buggy ride. But not until we get you those records to show your *Aenti.*"

He stood and extended a hand to her, helping her up from the grass.

Caleb pulled his buggy into the driveway of the B&B and Lila came out to greet them, her eyes red-rimmed. "I thought you were never coming back!" she said, her voice a little shaky

"I'm sorry," Casey said. "I had an errand to run in town. I should have let you know before I left."

"What was so important that it couldn't wait until later?" Lila asked, her eyes brimming with tears.

Casey handed her the envelope. "I had to get my birth records, and I went to Momma's gravesite."

"I wish I could have gone with you." Lila pulled Casey into her arms and rocked her back and forth with her sobs, Casey unable to hold in her emotions a moment longer.

"What is going on here?" Amy screeched. "Don't tell me you're falling for this impostor's lies, *mudder!*"

Lila pulled away from Casey and smiled, putting a hand under her chin. "She is no impostor; she looks just like Katie."

Casey wiped her face and sniffled. "You *knew* it was me all along?"

Lila nodded. *"Jah;* It was like looking into the past when I first saw you. I didn't say anything because I didn't want to spook you like an untamed horse. But then when you left and took your things with you, I was afraid I'd lost you all over again."

Casey looked up at her cousin, who threw down her crutches and crossed her arms defiantly while balancing on her walking cast. "I don't want another foster kid here, *mudder;* I'm tired of having to compete with them for your attention. I thought all that was over a few years ago when *she* would have turned eighteen. It was nice having you all to myself; I only wish *Dat* would have lived long enough to see the days when I was the only *kinner* in the *haus."*

Lila left Casey's side and went to her daughter. "I'm sorry if you felt that I didn't love you as much as I did *mei schweschder's* child. *Ach,* I never meant to hurt you; I suppose I let my guilt over shunning Katie drive me to make peace with her. The only way I saw to do that was to find the *boppli* she so desperately wanted me to help her with." Lila held out a hand to Casey, and she went to her.

Lila held both girl's hands and talked through her tears.

"At the time, I was newly married and expecting *mei* own *boppli,* and I didn't want to be bothered with the mistakes she'd made or the mess she'd made of her life by running off with the *Englisher.* I thought my warning was enough for her, but she was in love. She told me that he'd broken her heart because he was promised to marry another woman. I got a letter from her just weeks before she gave birth. I tried to find her but couldn't. Then one day the local police showed up at my door and told me she was at the city morgue—died in childbirth but gave up the *boppli* and signed a paper restricting me the right to raise the child. Knowing her, she did that to protect the child from being shunned the way she was. I couldn't get any information—not even if the child was a boy or girl. So that's why I started to take in foster kids—I couldn't live with the guilt of turning my back on *mei schweschder*. We were raised to shun those who didn't follow the rules, and I've always regretted it. I'm so sorry—for both of you girls. I didn't mean for either of you to have a hard life because of my mistake."

Lila turned to her daughter and smiled.

"Don't make the same mistakes I made with Katie; don't turn away your cousin. Life is for the living."

Tears filled Amy's eyes, and she buried herself in her mother's arms. Casey felt awkward and walked back toward Caleb's buggy.

"Can you take me back to the city?" she whispered, barely able to get the words out from her quivering lips.

"Wait!" Amy called. "Where are you going?"

Casey turned. "You two need some time—without me in the way. I think it would be best if I went back to the city."

She hopped up into the buggy, not daring to look her cousin or her aunt in the eye for fear her heart would break.

CHAPTER SIX

Amy hobbled over to the buggy, hollering for Caleb to stop. "I want you to stay!"

Casey looked up, searching Amy's eyes for any sign of sincerity in them, but couldn't tell for sure. "I'll just be in the way; you don't want me here—except to have someone around to blame for your hard life."

Amy held up her hand. "You're right! I blamed you; I was even jealous of you. I know it wasn't your fault your *mudder* left you in that orphanage, and I'm sorry she did; it might have been fun growing up with a cousin if things had been different, but you're here now."

Casey resisted the urge to roll her eyes. "Don't you have other cousins?"

"Jah, but we would be like *schweschders."*

Casey bit her bottom lip to steady it. Her heart could not take anymore disappointment.

Lila walked over to them and held out another hand to Casey. "Please stay; we *both* want you to."

Amy nodded. "*Mei mudder* is right. I'm sorry, *Cousin.*"

Casey hesitated. "What about Caleb?" she asked, looking at Amy. "He's asked me for a buggy ride—an *official* buggy ride—is that going to be a problem between you and me? Because I told him yes!"

Amy's face curled up into the biggest smile, and her eyes widened. "Then we will have a wedding to plan soon, *jah?"*

Casey felt her heart pounding harder than a stampede of horses. "Let me go on the first date—then I'll get back to you on that wedding stuff."

"If you're going to be Amish," Amy said. "You better understand the importance of a buggy ride—it signals the courting stage of a relationship. That stage can last a week, a month, or a year. It's up to the heart how long the courting lasts. But a wedding is sure to follow."

"Does this mean you're not mad about Caleb and me?"

Amy giggled. "*Nee,* we are cousins! Besides, Asa Hochstetler just got back from his cousin's *haus* in Ohio and came straight over to see me to bring me flowers because he'd heard about my leg. Anyway, he asked me if he could take me home from the singing on Sunday night, so we might be having *two* weddings this upcoming wedding season."

"Wedding season?" Casey asked.

Amy giggled and coaxed her cousin from the buggy. "If you are to embrace your heritage as Amish, you have a *lot* to learn!"

Lila pulled both girls into a hug, and they laughed and cried and hugged for several minutes.

"Let's get some lemonade and sit on the porch," Lila said. "We are long-overdue for a *familye* talk."

Casey followed Amy into the B&B, nearly forgetting all about Caleb until he cleared his throat behind her. She turned and smiled; she was too giddy for words. Not only did she have a new family, but she had a possible boyfriend, too.

He took her hand respectively and kissed her cheek. "I'll let you get acquainted with your *familye,* but I'll see you tomorrow bright and early," he said with a smile. "I wouldn't miss that strong *kaffi* or the pecan *kaffi* cake—or that smile, for anything in the world."

She giggled shyly. "Thank you."

Amy nudged her. "The way an Amish girl says *thank you* is *danki.*"

"*Danki,*" Casey said proudly.

"Let's sit on the porch and talk about those *English* clothes, Cousin," Amy said, looping her arm in Casey's.

Caleb waved a hand to her and ran out to his buggy, thinking that was his cue to give them some time for *girl-talk.*

"What's wrong with what I'm wearing?" Casey asked Amy after she watched Caleb turn out onto the main road in front of the B&B and disappear over the rise.

Amy shrugged. "Nothing—if you want to keep looking like an *Englisher.*"

Casey studied her cousin's plain lavender dress, her white linen apron and matching head covering. "Why do you wear that little white hat?"

"It's a prayer *kapp,*" Amy answered. "It is to keep our head covered. We only allow our husbands—when we are married—to see our hair down. But only in private."

"And the dresses?" Casey asked.

"For reasons of modesty and being feminine."

"Will I be expected to dress like you?" Casey asked.

"Not if you live as an *Englisher,*" Amy retorted. "But if you want to marry Caleb, you will have to live as Amish—and that means dressing and acting with humility."

Lila exited the house with lemonade on a tray, along with glasses, napkins, and a plate of cookies. Casey was glad for the break in the talk for a minute. Most of it was overwhelming her, and she didn't know why. Was she ready to give up electricity and motorized transportation? Not that she had a car, but it was the principle of it. She would gladly give up her room in the small house she shared with three roommates in the city—all girls she knew from the orphanage. It had almost felt as if she'd never left, but the group home had been all she could afford while she was in school. Would she have to give up her classes?

She watched her aunt Lila pouring lemonade for them and smiled when she handed her a glass and a napkin full of cookies. With so much to gain and very little to lose, how could the decision be anything besides staying here with her family and Caleb? With no real attachments in the city, staying here was a no-brainer. Would she be expected to pay her way? She suspected she'd help at the B&B but wondered about spending money. But then, what would she spend it on if all her needs were being met. The essentials like a roof over her head and food in her stomach were secondary to having a family and the love of a good man like Caleb.

"What did you do before you decided to come here to find us?" Lila asked.

"I was taking classes—to be a nurse," Casey answered. "I didn't like it very much, though. It's harder than you might think."

"Are you ready to give that up for the plain life?"

Casey took a sip of her lemonade and allowed the warm afternoon breeze to cool her; the scene was just as she'd imagined it. If plain living meant having a family and a relationship that could lead to marriage with Caleb, she was prepared to make the changes. "I was just thinking about that, and I believe I am ready."

Both women smiled at Casey, who was a bundle of nerves. How could a person be so nervous and so excited at the same time?

"I have a lot to learn, don't I?" Casey asked.

Lila reached over from the chair next to her where she sat with a smile so wide; she doubted it would leave her for some time. "*Jah,* we have a lot to teach you, but most of it you will probably pick up rather quickly. You already know how to cook; how did you learn such a thing if you spent all your life in that orphanage?"

"I volunteered for the cook's helper," she said, not wanting to tell her aunt the reasons behind such volunteer work. Any time they asked for volunteers for work, Casey was the first to sign up. It was the only way to stay occupied, and to keep the bullies at bay. While she worked, she was constantly under the watchful eyes of the staff, and those eyes had been like a protective shield around her.

"Well, it seems to have made you a well-rounded young lady," her aunt Lila said. "Do you also know how to sew?"

Casey nodded. "I can also crotchet; I made blankets for all the incoming babies while I was there."

Lila smiled. "*Gott* will truly reward you for such a labor of love."

"I held the babies and fed them too," Casey said proudly. "The staff allowed me to organize games for the younger kids and babysit them during the summer months."

"It sounds to me like you were a blessing to the wee ones there," Lila commented.

Casey hadn't thought of it that way before. She'd felt it a necessary burden in some ways—as if it was her responsibility to keep watch over the younger kids. Very few of them stayed long enough to get caught up in the problems that some of the *Lifers,* as she was called, had to endure. In the orphanage, if you were a *Lifer,* you didn't get out until your eighteenth birthday. Most of the *Lifers* were hard to place because of handicaps, or they were such trouble-makers that it caused them to be returned from foster care homes repeatedly. For Casey, she assumed it was her Amish background that kept her from being adopted. Aside from a couple of fights that she had not started, her record there was almost spotless; her background was the only thing that could have possibly held her back.

"Did I say something wrong?" Lila asked.

Casey looked up, forcing a smile, not realizing her expression had changed. "No, I was just thinking about all the kids that passed through there while I stayed until I turned eighteen."

Lila teared up again. "I'm so sorry you had to stay there; it must have been hard watching others getting families while you stayed there."

Casey nodded. "It was. But that part of my life is behind me." She smiled at her aunt and cousin. "I have a lifetime with family to look forward to. So, what shall we do first?"

"Would you like me to sew some dresses for you?" Amy asked.

Casey gulped as she studied the dresses her aunt and cousin wore. "Can I pick out any color I want?"

Amy giggled. "For your *gut* dresses, *jah,* but you will want the plain blue and brown for work. The darker colors keep you from getting stained. We can make you some white aprons and some black ones for working. I think you will find the dresses much cooler in this heat than those pants you're wearing."

Casey laughed. "I do like wearing dresses in the summer months, but what do you do in the winter time?"

"We wear thick, knit stockings under our dresses and it keeps us plenty warm," Amy said. "Sometimes we wear leggings if it's really cold."

"I have a pair of leggings," Casey said. "I don't have much with me; I left my other things in the city with my roommates. It isn't much more; just some clothing and some books, but I can get them next time I'm in town. I'll need to let the girls

know I'm not coming back to room with them—
that is if it's alright if I stay here. I'll continue to
work for the B&B if you need me to so I can pay
for my room and board."

Lila chuckled. "You don't need to pay for
your room and board; we're *familye*. We do pitch
in and help wherever needed—much like you did at
the orphanage—it's all volunteer."

Casey nodded and smiled. Yes, she was
going to enjoy being part of a family.

CHAPTER SEVEN

"Hold still, or I might stick you with a pin!" Amy said.

Casey continued to fidget. "Can you hurry up and pin it in place; I'm getting a cramp in my leg from standing here for so long."

Amy pulled a pin from the row she had stuck between her lips. "Last pin—and I'm done." She took the rest of the pins and put them back on the magnetized holder and then helped Casey out of the apron so she didn't pull apart the seams before Amy could sew them. It was not easy being still, but she didn't want to snag the delicate, organdy material. It was, after all, the apron she would wear this evening for her first official buggy ride date with Caleb. She'd practiced over, and over again, how to twist her hair up and pin it so it would fit nicely just below the organdy *kapp*. She had to admit, it was rather pretty, though plain. The wine-colored dress was going to be beautiful underneath the white apron, and she couldn't wait to see the expression on Caleb's face when he saw her in it.

Her heart thumped an extra beat at the thought of dressing in such feminine dresses all the time. At the orphanage, she was lucky to get hand-me-down trousers from some of the older boys, and it had made her feel like such a tom-boy. Dresses were forbidden though, and anything fancy was certainly not allowed. She was told it was to keep jealousy from cropping up and causing fights and theft. There was theft though; blankets in the winter time, pillows, and even cookies from another's tray were stolen quite often by the bigger, bullying kids. She gladly gave up the sweets, thanking them silently for keeping her from becoming plump and lazy like those who stole them.

It amazed her how quickly Amy could put together a dress with her mother. Aunt Lila had sewn the bodice while Amy had fashioned the sleeves and the skirt. Casey, herself, had sewn the hem since she was not as fast with the hand-stitching as they were.

She'd used an old treadle sewing machine at the orphanage, and though Lila had used that for the bodice of the dress, she wanted Casey to hand-stitch the hem, advising her that it would be good practice for the next quilting bee. She had no idea that all the quilts the Amish women made were hand-stitched. Amy had teased her that if the date went well this evening with Caleb, they'd be stitching a wedding ring pattern quilt for her dowry and a blue dress for her wedding. The thought of it had made her blush, but it had also made her think of the seriousness of her decision were Caleb was concerned.

Truthfully, she couldn't think of much besides Caleb all day. Sitting on the porch and sewing had kept her hands from being idle, but it had given her mind too much time to wander. He was a handsome man, but she'd suddenly been thrust into her heritage where she could expect to marry sooner than she would have if she'd remained living as an *Englisher*. She was suddenly someone *different* than she'd always thought of herself, but in a good way. Up until a few days ago, her only real concern had been how things would be when she finally met her family. Now that she had, her worries had turned to wondering if she'd ever want to return to being *English*.

Lord, show me what to do so I don't make a mistake or hurt Caleb; I think I already love him a little and I don't want to make a decision about him or my life here without thinking it through first. Keep me from being so nervous about my date with him.

"If you don't need me anymore so you can finish that," Casey said to Amy. "I have a couple of chores I'd promised your mother—*Aunt Lila*—before I get cleaned up for my um—*date.*"

Amy touched her arm. "You seem a little nervous now that it's been called a date. You seemed so sure about it yesterday; what changed?"

Casey didn't want to talk; she needed something—a chore—anything to keep her mind occupied so she didn't have to think anymore. It was giving her a headache.

Amy tapped the seat beside her on the porch swing. "Sit! I think you are nervous and I think you should ask me whatever question it is that I can see is on your mind."

Casey sighed and collapsed onto the swing, causing the chain to squeak. "Am I *expected* to marry Caleb if I go on the buggy ride with him?"

Amy giggled and snorted. "Is that all you're worried about?"

Casey scowled. "What do you mean, is that all? That's a *big* thing!"

"You never thought about marriage before?"

Casey could feel her cheeks heating. "I've never really *dated* before—unless you count hanging out with a group of people where some of them were guys."

"You've never been on a date alone with a *mann?*"

Casey shook her head and lowered her gaze. "Nope!"

"I thought all *English* girls were—you know—advanced—as far as dating goes."

Casey shook her head again. "Not me! Up until I came here a few days ago, I've been passing the time until I could come here to meet my family. Now that I'm here, I suddenly find myself having the freedom to pursue a relationship with a guy I'm interested in. I'm not sure how to react. I really like him—I might have already fallen in love with him, but I've *never* given any thought to marrying. My whole life has been on hold until I met you and your mother."

"Since you're here and we settled our differences—*my differences*—you can relax and enjoy your life," Amy said. "And that means allowing yourself to fall in love and eventually get married and have a *familye* of your own. We will always be your *familye* now, and we will always be here. So enjoy your life and see what the future has in store for you. If it isn't with Caleb, even though I suspect he's the one, you can date someone else. You are *not* required to marry him if you take a buggy ride with him. But if you want to continue to see him, you are considered courting, and that almost always ends with a marriage. Not always; sometimes things go wrong, but if you're meant to be together, you'll know."

Casey breathed a little easier. "Thank you, *Cousin!*"

"Ach, any time I can be of help," Amy said. "I sort of owe you since I almost sent you away permanently."

"You have nothing you owe me," Casey said. "I should have been honest when I first came here instead of pretending to be here for the job—although I'm glad I got the job."

Both girls laughed, and it made Casey's heart warm up to her cousin. Like herself, Amy wasn't as tough as she pretended to be.

Casey admired her reflection even though Amy warned her it was considered prideful to practice vanity. With mirrors only in the guestrooms, she had to stand on the edge of the bathtub to see the full length of the dress in the bathroom mirror that connected to her room at the B&B. Amy had shown her that there were no mirrors in the living quarters out back of the property she'd referred to as a *dawdi haus*. She supposed that was one of the reasons Amy had told her to practice twisting her hair without the use of a mirror. Would the mirror be taken from her eventually? She hoped not because she enjoyed her reflection so much now despite the fact Amy told her it would eventually lose its luster. Casey found the notion hard to believe as she admired the dress she'd helped to sew, but did see the logic in her cousin's explanations of such things.

As a wife, she supposed it would no longer matter what she looked like on the outside as long as she didnt change on the inside. It wasn't the same in the vain *English* world where people seemed to place more importance on the outward appearance. For that reason, she didn't dare admit to Amy that she found Caleb extremely handsome. Truthfully, if she didn't know what he looked like;

he would still be appealing to her because of his kind heart. After all, she probably wouldn't be here now if it hadn't been for the kindness he'd shown her that day he'd given her that first buggy ride.

Casey giggled thinking about that day that seemed like it was years ago, though it had only been a few days. So much had happened to her already and she'd learned more in the past few days than she felt she had her entire life so far.

A knock at the bathroom door startled her, and she nearly slipped off the edge of the tub. Catching herself, she took one last peak in the mirror before climbing down and opening the door.

"Caleb is here!" Amy said with a smile.

Casey resisted the urge to ask her cousin how she looked. Instead, she stole one last glance at her hair that was tucked neatly underneath the white organdy *kapp*.

"Ach, you look fine, and Caleb is going to find you irresistible!"

"Amy!" Casey said with exasperation. "I thought you said vanity was prideful."

"It is—but you're not fully Amish yet, so I'm sure it's alright—just this once."

Casey giggled and hugged her cousin.

"Thank you—I mean, *danki*; I needed to hear that."

"Get going!" Amy warned. "You don't want to keep a *mann* like Caleb waiting—not when he's as devoted to you as a *mann* could be. He's wearing his Sunday best for you!"

Casey felt her heart skip a beat, the anticipation making her shake. She drew in a deep breath and went toward the stairs. As she descended slowly, her eyes fixed on Caleb, checking him from head to toe.

Atop his sandy hair, sat a dressy black hat. A white button-up dress shirt tucked neatly into a pair of black dress pants held up by a pair of suspenders. The contours of his chest were visible when he removed his hat in reverence to her presence. What a gentlemanly gesture. Casey felt her breath hitch as she closed the space between them, Caleb remaining at the landing of the stairwell unmoving, but his smile said everything she could see he was thinking.

Yes, she was thinking the same thing.

CHAPTER EIGHT

Caleb walked out with Casey on his arm, thinking he was the luckiest *mann* in the world. She'd taken his breath away when she'd come down the staircase only moments ago. He'd never seen a more beautiful Amish woman than Casey turned out to be, and that pleased him. He'd wrung his hands most of the day wondering if he was doing the right thing by asking her for a buggy ride. Then there was the whole worry about whether she would fit in, or if she'd change her mind altogether and leave the community. He'd nearly driven himself mad with all the what-ifs.

Now, she was on his arm and about to get into his buggy, and all his worries had faded away. Judging by the way she looked, he'd have to say she was prepared for a long-term stay in the community and that gave him reason to relax. He wouldn't compliment her, so as not to get her used to it, but he hoped his smile conveyed his pleasure with her appearance.

Caleb assisted Casey into his courting buggy and then hopped up beside her, sitting close enough that his leg touched hers. It was a test that most of the youth used to see if the girl was interested in him enough that she would not move her leg. It gave him such a thrill when he picked up the reins, and she moved in a little closer and looped her arm back in his.

Jah, she's interested!

He set his horse at a slow trot, prepared to take his time driving to the lake where the youth parked their buggies under the stars and talked about their futures together. "Is the lakefront alright with you?" he asked, making sure she wouldn't think him presumptuous for taking her there. "I packed *kaffi* and cookies *mei mamm* baked; I thought we could sit there and enjoy the view—and the stars, of course."

She giggled. "Is the lake where everyone around here takes their dates?"

"*Jah,*" he said seriously. "It's a small lake—owned by the community. During the day, we have Sunday picnics there and usually congregate there for working bees—unless it's for a barn-raising. Then, we end up on the barn owner's property, and the women set up food for the *menner* while they work."

"Amy filled me in on some of that—and the lake—for dating purposes. There isn't much else to do around here except go to Sunday night singings, which she also told me about, and I'm not so sure I'm ready for that."

Caleb cleared his throat. "So you're on to me, then!"

"What do you mean?"

He cleared his throat again, feeling his heart racing. "You understand that I wanted this date to be *special*."

She nodded and smiled. "It's special to me, too."

His heart sped up even faster if that was possible. Would Casey agree to marry him if he asked her? Would she object to him kissing her? He wanted to kiss her from the moment his gaze met with hers when she'd walked down the stairs at the B&B in her new Amish dress. He wanted to tuck his arm around her and kiss her now, but he was driving. It was tough to keep his concentration on the road, but he was grateful the horse knew the way, and it wasn't too much further.

He supposed he could wait until they reached the lake.

Casey felt her breath catch in her throat when Caleb parked his buggy in a private spot in front of the lake, the moonlight reflecting in the ripples of the water. It was a pleasant night, and the lightning bugs illuminated the tree branches like little fairies keeping a watch over the lake. Frogs croaked and splashed as they hopped from one lily pad to another.

Casey looked out at the expanse of the lake. "It's so peaceful out here; you can hear the frogs splashing in the lake."

Caleb pointed toward the sky. "Look; a shooting star."

"Make a wish!" Casey said, closing her eyes and concentrating on her wish.

After she finished, she opened her eyes and looked over at Caleb, who was staring at her.

"What did you wish for?" he asked.

She gasped. "I can't tell you!"

He chuckled. "Why not? Was it about me?'

Her face heated. "If you tell what you wished for then it won't come true."

He leaned against the back of the buggy and tucked his arm around her. "Says who?"

Casey straightened when his arm made contact with her mid-back; the warmth of his skin permeated her dress.

"I don't know exactly, but everyone knows you're supposed to keep your wish a secret, or it won't come true."

She relaxed a little and allowed herself to lean back enough to feel his arm behind her again. Just knowing it was there sent tingles all the way to her toes.

"I'll tell you mine if you tell me yours!" he said.

"No!" she squealed. "It won't come true."

He scooted closer to her, which made her warm all over.

"I'm afraid if I *don't* tell you it won't come true," he confessed.

"Why do you have to tell *me?*"

He smiled, and it made her let out a little sigh.

"Because it's about *you!*"

"Then I *really* don't want you to tell me!"

He smiled and moved closer. "But I *must* tell you, or I'm afraid it will have the opposite effect, and it will *never* come true."

Her hands flew to her ears, and she plugged a finger in each one. "Don't tell me—please don't tell me!"

"I wished I could kiss you," he said, moving nearer her.

His face was so close to hers she could see the reflection of the moon in his eyes.

"Now, it surely won't come true!" she said, suppressing a giggle.

He closed the space between them and tucked his other arm around her. "But you can *make* it come true if you kiss me."

Her breath hitched. "I couldn't; it wouldn't be fair to everyone else who follows the rules about keeping wishes to yourself." Her heart beat faster than if she'd run all the way to the lake.

He moved his head to the side and touched his lips to her cheek, causing her breath to hitch once more. "I think if you kiss me it will break the spell for everyone who's ever told, and all their wishes will suddenly come true."

Her eyes fluttered closed when his lips touched her neck. "Wouldn't that cause an overload of wishes?" she asked, trying her best to keep her focus on the conversation and not on his lips as they traveled down her neck to her collarbone. She sighed dreamily, unable to think straight.

"I don't care," Caleb said. "Right now, all I care about is kissing you."

He paused and moved his face so close to hers their noses nearly touched. Casey felt his warm, minty breath on her lips just before they touched hers.

The hair on the back of her neck raised and gooseflesh prickled her arms and traveled down her spine like someone had plugged her into a wall socket. Caleb tasted of mint leaves, and his musky scent made her swoon.

His lips swept across hers with the graceful movement of a ballet dancer. It was breath-taking and exciting, and it was exactly what she'd wished for.

  Caleb couldn't help himself; he had to kiss Casey when the perfect opportunity fell in his lap. He couldn't help himself because he was falling for her. He suspected her resistance was because she'd wished for the same thing. When she deepened the kiss, he knew he'd guessed right. Now, as he held Casey in his arms, he thanked God for the shooting star and the wish that brought them together in such an intimate way. If it were up to him, he'd stay out here all night and kiss her under the stars, but his next wish, if they should see another shooting star, would be to marry Casey.

CHAPTER NINE

Casey sat on the porch letting the breeze tickle the back of her neck where stray auburn hair fluttered from under her prayer *kapp*. She stared at the smile that tipped the corners of her mother's mouth in the faded photograph. She looked happy, and that was important to Casey. The woman might not have lived long, but she looked incredibly content to be in the arms of the man pictured with her. Could he be Casey's father? If so, what had happened between them that drove her mother to the orphanage to give her up for adoption?

"When I got that picture from her, she didn't tell me they were dating, but I suspected as much," her aunt Lila interrupted her thoughts.

Casey looked up from the picture that was like looking in the mirror. No wonder Aunt Lila recognized her right away.

"Did she tell you anything about him?"

Lila frowned. "Only his first name; Nicolo. She told me in the last letter she wanted me to help her come home, but I knew it wasn't possible in her condition. We both knew she would be shunned for her indiscretion with the young *mann*, and she didn't give a forwarding address." Lila dipped her hand into the small box once more and pulled out a couple of letters. "You can read them yourself; she gave no clue where she was."

Casey looked at the faded postmark. It came from the city—where the orphanage is. Had she happened upon the orphanage by chance? She studied the picture a little more closely, taking her focus from her mother's face to the background. "I know this place!" she blurted excitedly. "Look; he's wearing an apron! I wonder if he worked at the bakery. Maybe the owners would remember. It's a family-owned place—Romano's Bakery. If his first name is Nicolo, I'd be willing to bet his last name is Romano, and that could be his family's bakery. If not, they might remember him if I bring the picture with me."

"Don't get your hopes up," Lila warned her. "This picture was taken more than twenty-one years ago."

"I have to go!" she said. "It's my only hope to find out what happened—what really happened to my mother."

Lila smiled. "I understand. I'd like to know too."

Casey stared at the older man behind the counter and then back at the picture in her hand. Except for a little gray at his temples and wrinkles around his eyes, she was certain he was the same man.

She walked in; the bells on the door alerted him she was there, and she suddenly wondered if she should have worn *English* clothes instead of the Amish dress and *kapp*. She'd asked Caleb to stay outside with the buggy while she went into the bakery herself—just in case it was a dead-end.

The man looked up and stared; he seemed to freeze in place. She moved in closer, noticing the stricken look across his face. But then his eyes brightened, and a hopeful smile crossed his lips as he came around the counter near her.

"You look just like your mother did the first time she walked in through that door," he said, his lower lip quivering.

"You know who I am?" Casey asked.

The man nodded his head and began to blubber, and that made Casey cry.

"By the look of you, I'd have to say you're Katie Lapp's daughter; I think that makes you *my* daughter, too. Am I right in assuming this?" he asked.

"Yes," Casey said. "I'm here because I want to know what happened between you and my mother all those years ago."

He leaned against the counter. "What is it you want to know? I'll tell you everything I can."

"How did you meet her?" Casey asked. "She was Amish."

"My mother hired her when she walked in one day asking for a job. My mother knew the Amish were wonderful bakers and thought it would be a good combination for the bakery," he said. "It didn't take me long to fall in love with her. She was funny and smart, and she taught me how to bake a lot of things our bakery didn't normally sell." He pointed to a tray of cookies in the display case. "That is your mother's recipe; it's one of our best-sellers.

"Why do you still make them and sell them after all these years?" Casey demanded.

He let out a sigh, his face turning red. "I know it sounds silly, but I never got over your mother. My father didn't approve of my relationship with your mother," he said sadly. "He practically had me married off to the daughter of his business partner from the time we were infants. He wanted his bakery business to *stay in the family,* and he didn't believe that would happen if I married outside of my Italian background. He even disowned me when I refused to marry the girl, but my mother asked me to return after he had a heart attack. Someone had to run the bakery."

"You never married?" Casey asked.

He shook his head. "No; there was no one who could replace your mother in my heart. I went looking for her a few months after she left because I couldn't stand to be without her any longer, but no one would answer any of my questions. I told myself it was for the better."

"That doesn't explain why she left in the first place," Casey said, "She was pregnant with me; why didn't you marry her or run away with her?"

"We had an awful fight the night she left because I wanted to marry her but my parents were trying to force me to marry their friend's daughter," he said. "I'd been asking her since we found out she was pregnant, and she'd promised to think about it. We were both too young to be getting married and raising a child, but I was willing. She didn't want to get between my family and me. She said she wanted to go back to the Amish community to her own family; she told me I wouldn't be welcome there. She said she missed her family so much; she used to cry at night, and it made me feel bad. I loved her enough to let her go because I thought that was what she wanted. Did she end up marrying that Yoder fellow when she went back to the community?"

"Her sister, Lila, married the Yoder *fellow,*" Casey said, annoyance in her tone.

"She didn't marry, then?" he asked.

His tone sounded almost hopeful, and she was being snarky.

Casey's heart beat fast and hard, a lump in her throat making it difficult to breathe. "You mean you *really* don't know what happened to her after she left here?"

His expression became alarmed. "I'm guessing your mother must have told you where to find me," he said nervously.

"She never said a word to me that I can remember; she died giving birth to me!" Casey said angrily.

The color drained from his cheeks, and he stumbled backward into one of the chairs in the small dining area. Tears filled his eyes as he looked up at Casey.

"Who—um—who raised you?" he asked.

"The state of Indiana!" Casey said bluntly. "I was raised in the orphanage where she left me after she died there giving birth to me."

She knew how angry she sounded, but looking at this man, she realized just how much she'd missed out on while growing up. She'd missed out on having a dad and a family. Had her mother thought that was what was best for her? She knew from seeing other kids getting adopted throughout the years that it had been the best for them, but she'd somehow slipped through the cracks and didn't get that life.

"I'm so sorry!" he said, his voice shaky. "Why didn't anyone find me so I could take care of you?"

"She didn't tell anyone who my father was before she died," Casey answered. "She didn't put a name on my birth records; why would she do that?"

Casey watched her father cross the room and turned over the sign on the door to say *Closed*.

"I don't know; it makes no sense. Unless she thought I'd married Maria after she left!" he said, running a hand through his dark hair. He removed his apron and set it on the tall counter above the display case. "I had no idea she was going to give you up so she could go back; I didn't know that was part of the plan. If I had, I'd have found a way to raise you myself."

Why was Casey so unhappy? Aunt Lila had welcomed her into her family, and this man seemed happy to see her. Was it really that easy to accept the blessing she had now? Granted, it hadn't come when she'd wanted it most, but sometimes, for reasons she didn't understand, God had made her wait. Now that the blessing had finally come, she would not waste a single moment of it.

Casey looked into her father's sad, sincere eyes while he stared at her mother's picture.

He was hurting too, and she believed him.

She was no longer Casey Harper, the orphan; she was Casey Romano, and she had a family.

Casey brought Caleb into the bakery and stood in front of her father. "I want you to meet Mr.—uh, what should I call you?"

The man smiled, crinkles forming at the corners of his eyes. "You can call me Nicolo if you want to."

She thought about it for a minute and crinkled her nose. "Can I try calling you *Dad?*" she asked timidly.

His eyes widened, and so did his smile. "I'd like that."

Casey giggled. "In that case, *Dad;* I'd like you to meet Caleb."

The two men shook hands. "It's a pleasure to meet you, Sir," Caleb said.

Nicolo put a hand on Caleb's shoulder. "Hey, what's with all this *Sir,* stuff?" he asked. "I get the feeling you'll be calling me Dad soon, too."

Casey blushed.

"I hope so," Caleb said, smiling at her.

Casey felt her heart skip a beat; was he going to propose soon?

CHAPTER TEN

Casey snuggled close to Caleb on the way home. It had been a long day of visiting with her father. He'd shared so many pictures and stories of her mother, it eased the pain of losing her—something that none of them could have prevented.

"Are you too tired to take a ride out to the lake?" Caleb asked.

Her heart sped up again with anticipation that this could be the time; was she ready for a proposal so soon? Thinking of her mother, she didn't want to make the same mistake she'd made in turning away from the man who wanted to marry her. She wanted to live and experience all those things her mother didn't have a chance to do. If he asked; Casey's answer would be yes. There was no doubt in her mind that God had brought her whole life together, and it had started with a simple buggy ride.

Casey sat on the porch swing with Caleb and watched her widowed Aunt Lila talking to her father out in the garden. It made her happy that her aunt had welcomed him into the family. The two of them had spent so much time together the past couple of weeks that she began to wonder if they wouldn't be married this wedding season too. It did Casey's heart good to see the two of them together, though she knew their connection to her mother was what brought them together, and it had seemed to heal both their broken hearts. Was that all part of God's plan?

It seemed funny to Casey that she was so much like her mother even though she'd not been raised by her, but she supposed her mother's qualities were engraved in her DNA, and that was not something that would change. Though she had a lot of her father's qualities too, it amazed her that every time her father or her aunt mentioned something about her mother, she didn't have to think twice to know the connection she had with the woman. And if she wanted to feel close to her, she didn't have to look far; all she had to do was look in the mirror and inside her own heart, a place her mother would always be.

THE END

Made in the USA
Coppell, TX
20 February 2023

13136972R00073